Polo, the Guide Dog Puppy

Story by Jackie Tidey

Illustrations by Dede Putra

Contents

Chapter 1

Playing with Polo

Archie played with Polo
every day after school.

"Polo always does what I tell him,"
Archie said to Dad.
"He will be a good guide dog one day."

"Archie," said Dad.
"I had a phone call today
from the Guide Dog School.
On Friday, Polo is going to leave us.
He is ready to be trained as a guide dog."

"Oh, Dad," said Archie.
"I don't want Polo to go away from here."

"Polo has a big job to do," said Dad.
"At the Guide Dog School
he will do more training.
Then he will be ready
to live with someone who cannot see.
Polo will be a big help every day."

"Polo will be very good at that,"
said Archie.

Chapter 2

Don't Be Sad, Archie

Mum came home from work.

Archie told her that Polo
was going to be leaving them on Friday.

"Don't be sad, Archie," said Mum.
"We have had a great time with Polo.
And you have helped him a lot."

"Polo is not scared
of going to new places now,"
said Archie.

"And if dogs bark at Polo,
he does not bark at them,"
said Mum.

"But I am still sad
that Polo is going away," said Archie.

Chapter 3

Goodbye, Polo

On Friday morning,
Archie gave Polo a hug.

Then Mum put Polo in the car.
Archie and Dad waved goodbye to them.

After school, Archie saw that Dad
had washed Polo's dog house.
He had painted it, too.

But Polo wasn't there,
so Archie went inside and watched TV.

Mum was late home from work that day.
She called to Archie and Dad.
“Please come outside to the car,” she said.
“I need some help.”

Archie saw a basket
in the back of Mum's car.
He could see a small black puppy
in the basket.

"Is this little puppy for us?"
Archie asked Mum and Dad.

"Yes he is," said Mum.
"You were very good at training Polo.
So the Guide Dog School
wants you to help them again."